I0813555

MY FAVORITE DOG

DACHSHUNDS

by Anna Davison, MS

Dog Expert: Beth Adelman, MS

Former editor, *American Kennel Club Gazette*

Kaleidoscope

Minneapolis, MN

The Quest for Discovery Never Ends

This edition first published in 2021 by Kaleidoscope Publishing, Inc.

For information regarding permission, write to
Kaleidoscope Publishing, Inc.
6012 Blue Circle Drive
Minnetonka, MN 55343

Library of Congress Control Number
2020936278

ISBN
978-1-64519-439-2 (library bound)
978-1-64519-451-4 (ebook)

Printed in the United States of America.

FIND ME IF YOU CAN!

Bigfoot lurks within one of the images in this book. It's up to you to find him!

TABLE OF CONTENTS

Introduction

Here Comes a Dachshund!

Amy looked at the pile of blankets in her room. She saw a pointy **snout** poke out. A nose twitched. One eye opened. Fred was awake at last!

Amy watched her dog crawl out of his bed. Two big paws stretched out, pulling a very long body. Fred slowly stood up. He shook himself, his ears flapping. Wagging his long tail, he trotted toward her.

Amy first met Fred when he was just a wiggly little puppy. He was living at an **animal shelter**. It was love at first sight. Amy couldn't resist Fred's long, thin body. She loved his stubby legs. Amy had found a new friend!

FUN FACT

Some people call Dachshunds Doxies for short.

Chapter 1

The Story of Dachshunds

Dachshunds were first bred in Germany hundreds of years ago. They used to hunt badgers. *Dachs* means "badger" in German. *Hund* means "dog." That's how Dachshunds got their name.

FUN FACT
In the late 1800s, Queen Victoria helped make Dachshunds popular in Great Britain.

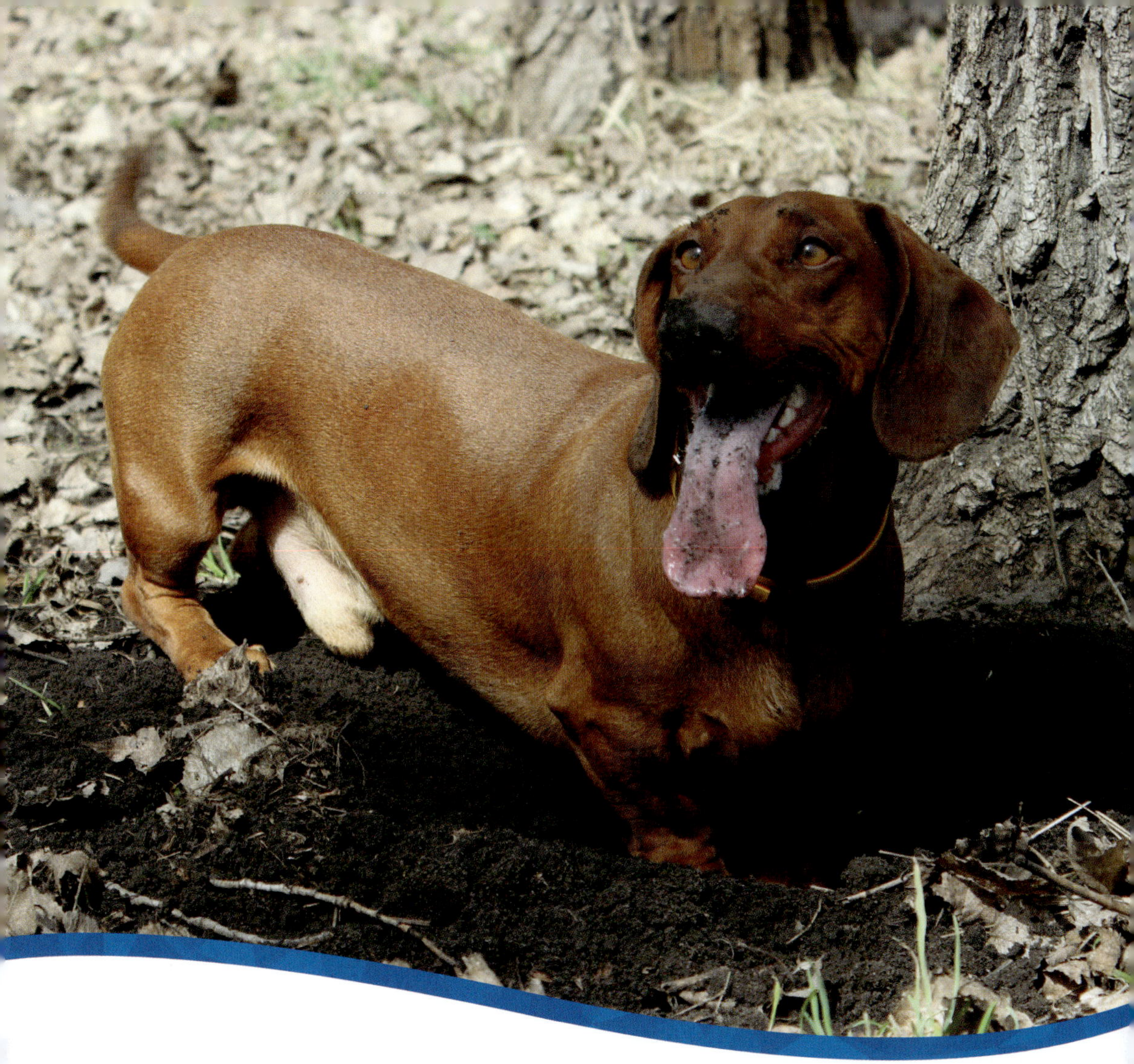

A Dachshund's shape isn't an accident. Badgers are small animals who hide in underground holes. The hunting dogs' long bodies and short legs helped them squeeze into small spaces.

They also have oversized front feet that are great for digging. They used those paws to chase badgers in their underground homes.

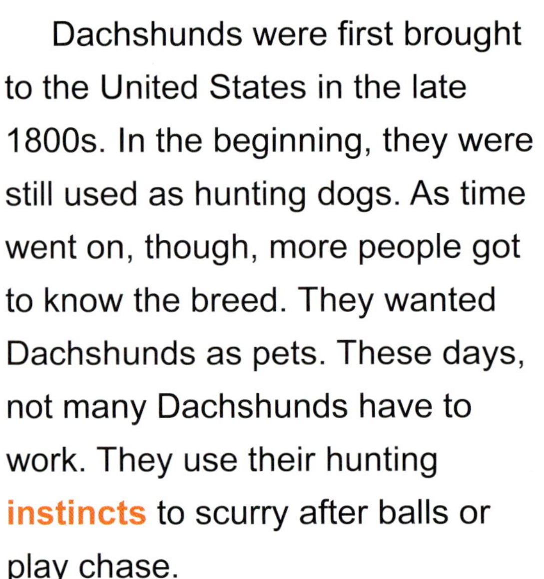

Dachshunds were first brought to the United States in the late 1800s. In the beginning, they were still used as hunting dogs. As time went on, though, more people got to know the breed. They wanted Dachshunds as pets. These days, not many Dachshunds have to work. They use their hunting **instincts** to scurry after balls or play chase.

OLYMPIC DOG!

A Dachshund named Waldi was the **mascot** of the Summer Olympic Games held in Munich, Germany, in 1972. **Marathon** runners followed a route shaped like a Dachshund!

Dog breeds are divided into groups. Dachshunds are part of the Hound Group. Hounds are dogs who were originally used for hunting. Fred is a scent hound. That means he uses his great sense of smell to sniff out **prey**—or treats! Because Dachshunds are such short dogs, their noses are always close to the ground. They are always ready to follow the faintest scent. They use their super sense of smell to find animals in dark holes. Their long ears help push the scents toward their noses.

WHERE DACHSHUNDS COME FROM

NORWAY

SWEDEN

SCOTLAND

North Sea

IRELAND

ENGLAND

GERMANY

FRANCE

Atlantic Ocean

Germany

ITALY

SPAIN

FUN FACT

Dachshunds come in 15 different color combinations.

Chapter 2
Looking at a Dachshund

When Amy takes Fred for a walk, people often stop to fuss over him. He does look a little odd. He looks like he's been stretched out! His body is almost three times as long as he is tall.

Fred is a Miniature Dachshund. Like the original Dachshunds from Germany, he has a short, smooth coat.

Fred's coat is a rich red color. Dachshunds can also be many shades of brown, black, gray, or white. They may have patches of different colors or spots. They can even be a stripy pattern called brindle.

DIFFERENT DACHSHUNDS

Dachshunds come in two sizes and three kinds of coats. Miniature Dachshunds are about as tall as a small cat. Standard Dachshunds are larger. The different sizes were bred to hunt different sized animals.

Dachshunds with short coats like Fred are called Smooth (right). Wirehaired Dachshunds (below) have stiff hair to protect them in thorny bushes. Longhaired Dachshunds (top) were bred to work in cold weather.

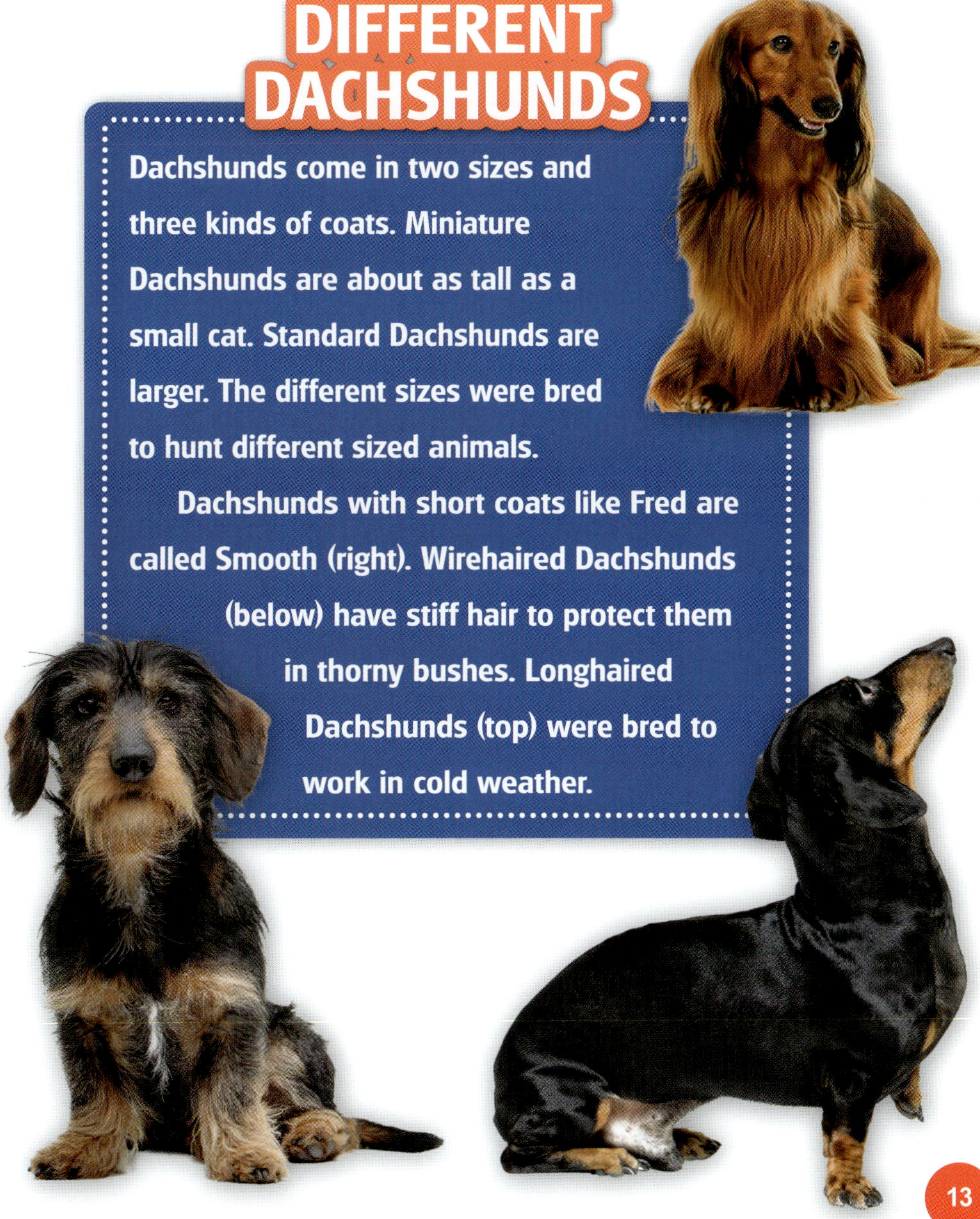

THE DACHSHUND

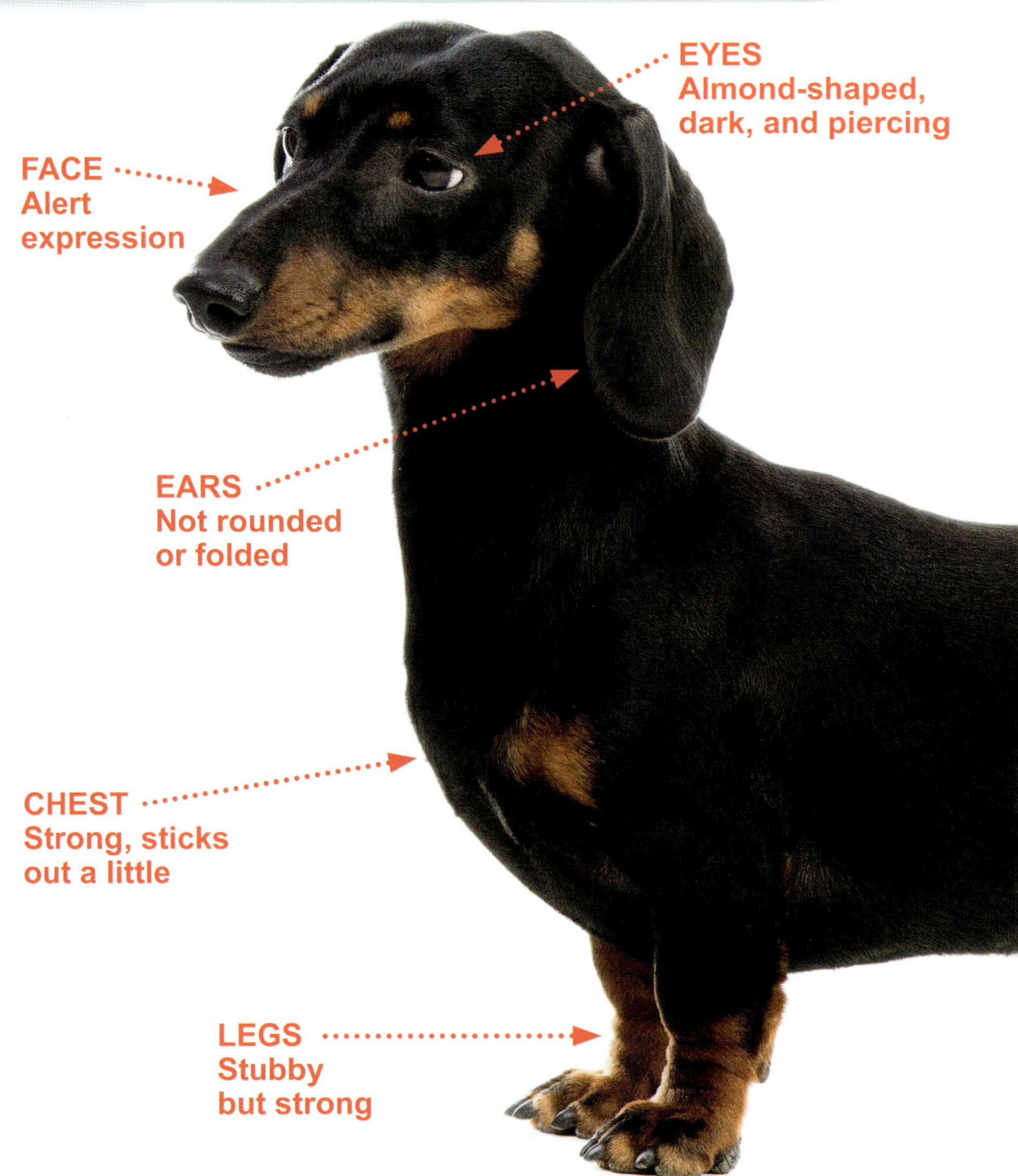

MINIATURE

HEIGHT*:
5–6 in. (12.7–15.2 cm)

WEIGHT:
up to 11 lbs. (up to 4.9 kg)

STANDARD

HEIGHT*:
8–9 in. (20.3–22.9 cm)

WEIGHT:
16–32 lbs. (7.2–14.5 kg)

The height of a dog is measured from the top of the shoulder, not from the top of the head.

Chapter 3

Meet a Dachshund!

Dachshunds may be small dogs, but they don't seem to realize it. Fred isn't afraid to challenge bigger dogs. His bark is quite loud. When someone comes to the front door, Fred lets everyone know. Dachshunds make good guard dogs!

Dachshunds need training, exercise, and play. If they get bored, they make up their own games. These games might include things you don't want your dog to do. They may chew on things or bark a lot. They love to dig, too. Fred sometimes tries to tunnel under the fence in the backyard. Amy works with Fred every day to train him to do the right things.

Dachshunds are very playful and determined. Fred loves to chase a ball around the yard. If it rolls under a bush, Fred grabs at the ball with his big front paws. He won't stop until he's got it back!

FUN FACT
Dachshunds could be athletes. They may be short, but they are strong and active.

Balls aren't the only thing Fred enjoys chasing. He's got the same hunting instinct as the earliest Dachshunds. He'll sniff his way through the yard. He'll follow the faint scents of small animals. He will chase squirrels and birds, too. He may be short, but he loves to run!

Fred knows a few tricks, too. He will lift up a paw to shake or roll over to show off his belly. Amy started training Fred when he was just a puppy. It's best to begin early! Fred loves to work with Amy and do what she asks. Then she gives him a treat and tells him what a good boy he is!

Most of all, Fred just likes to be by Amy's side. When it's time to relax, he loves to curl himself into her lap.

FUN FACT

Dog training tip: Praise good behavior quickly so your dog knows it has done well!

Chapter 4

Caring for a Dachshund

Amy sometimes finds Fred sitting in the kitchen. He is staring at his food bowl. Amy knows what he's hinting at. Like a typical Dachshund, Fred loves food.

He gets fed twice a day. That doesn't stop Fred from asking for more. Sometimes he begs for extras from the dinner table. Amy knows it's not a good idea to give in to him. Dachshunds need a healthy diet. If they get too heavy, their long backs can start to hurt.

To help keep Fred trim and happy, Amy walks him around the neighborhood every day. He also gets more exercise playing in the yard.

Because of their long spines, Dachshunds can get sore backs. Be gentle! They can hurt themselves just by jumping too far or too enthusiastically.

Fred's healthy diet helps keep his short coat nice and shiny. Every few days, Amy brushes him. Dachshunds with longer coats need to be groomed more often.

Once a week, Amy gives Fred a bath. She uses dog shampoo and warm water to rub him clean. Fred shakes himself off to dry. His long ears spin around his head. Drops of water go flying all over the bathroom! Amy finishes drying him with a soft towel.

TREAT OR NOT TO TREAT?

Dogs love treats. Make sure they don't get too many! Healthy treats are a great way to train your dog. They can be a reward for doing something right. But too many treats can be unhealthy. Choose treats that are tasty and good for your dog.

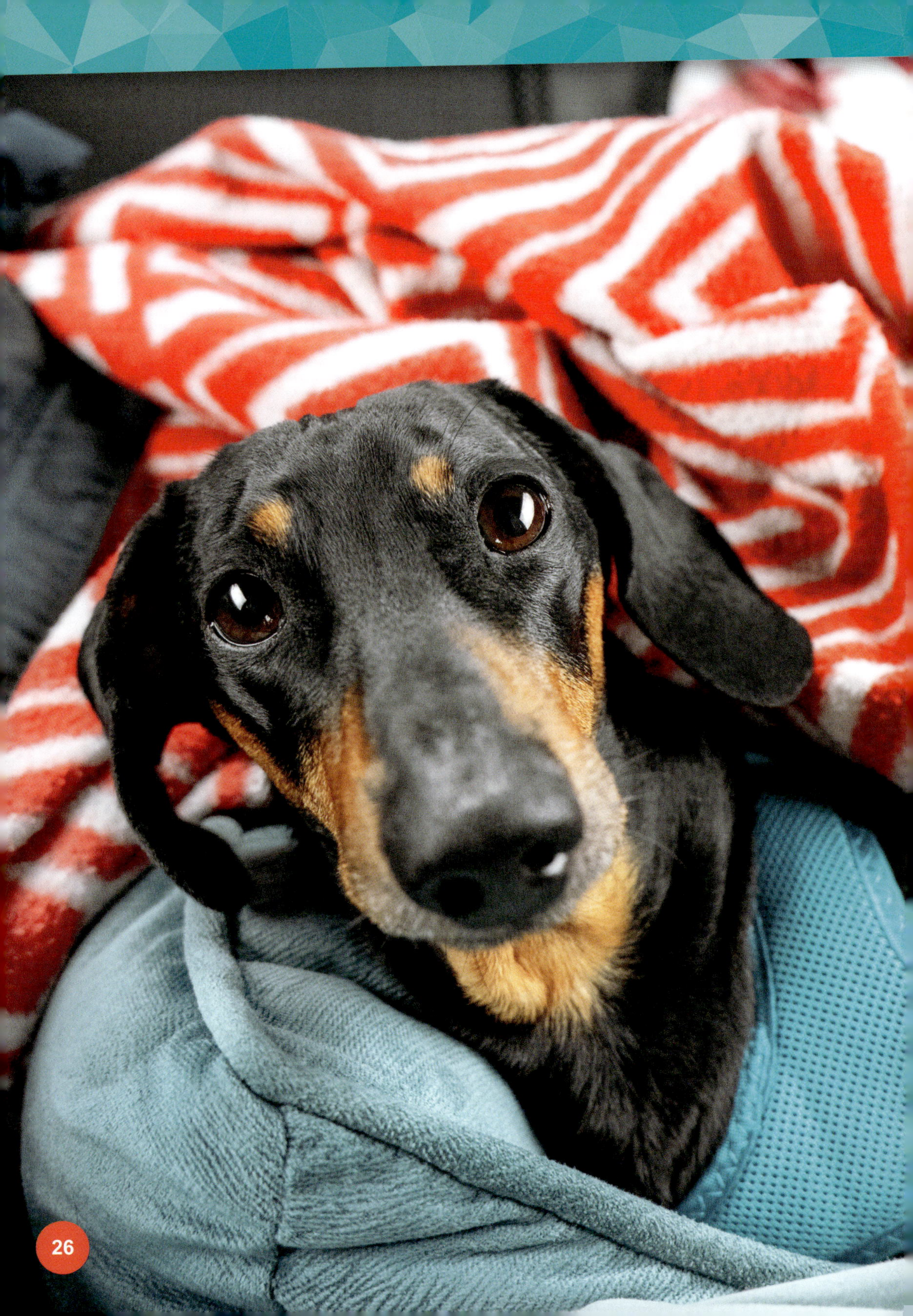

After playing, walking, and cuddling, Amy puts Fred to bed. She lays some cozy blankets around him. He likes to burrow into them. He is acting like the first Dachshunds who dug into the dirt to find prey. "Sweet dreams," she tells him.

In the morning, Amy returns to find a small mound of blankets. Fred must be in there somewhere! Then she sees a little black nose peeking out. It twitches, picking up the scent of breakfast. Time to get up, Fred!

Like people, dogs need to have clean teeth. Every day, Amy brushes Fred's with special dog toothpaste.

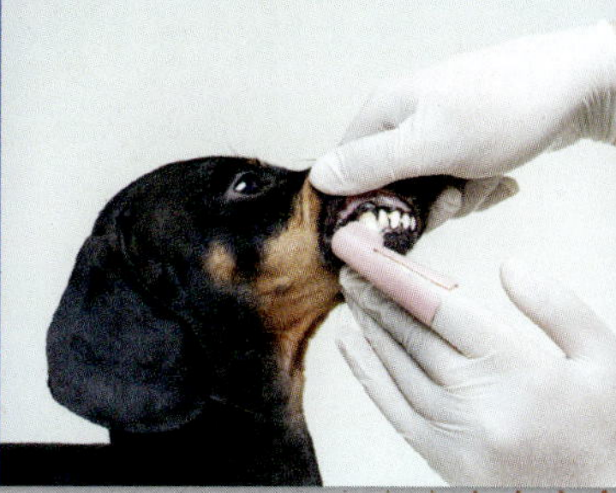

BEYOND

THE BOOK

After reading the book, it's time to think about what you learned. Try the following exercises to jumpstart your ideas.

RESEARCH

FIND OUT MORE. There is so much more to find out about Dachshunds. Visit the American Kennel Club's site to research Dachshunds. Or look for a Dachshunds Club in your area. You can meet other people who love your favorite breed!

CREATE

TIME FOR ART. How long can you make a Dachshund? Use your imagination and draw a super-long Dachshund. Put your XXL Dachshund in a fun place, like at the beach or at a mall. What crazy situations would happen if your gigantic dog actually went out in the world?

DISCOVER

LOTS OF BREEDS. This book is about your favorite dog breed. But there are hundreds more around the world. Visit the AKC site or those of other dog organizations. What other breeds can you discover? Which breeds are related to your favorite? What is the most interesting new breed you have discovered?

GROW

HELP OUT! Animal shelters can be great places to volunteer. Contact a shelter near you and find out if you can help. Or can your family donate food or gear to help rescue dogs? Find out why dogs end up in shelters. Is there anything you can do to help them find homes?

Visit www.ninjaresearcher.com/4392 to learn how to take your research skills and book report writing to the next level!

SEARCH LIKE A PRO
Learn about how to use search engines to find useful websites.

FACT OR FAKE?
Discover how you can tell a trusted website from an untrustworthy resource.

TEXT DETECTIVE
Explore how to zero in on the information you need most.

SHOW YOUR WORK
Research responsibly—learn how to cite sources.

WRITE

GET TO THE POINT
Learn how to express your main ideas.

PLAN OF ATTACK
Learn prewriting exercises and create an outline.

DOWNLOADABLE REPORT FORMS

Further Resources

BOOKS

Adelman, Beth. *Good Dog!: Dog Care for Kids.* Mankato, MN: Child's World, 2014.

Beal, Abigail. *I Love My Dachshund.* PowerKids Press, 2011.

Schuh, Mari. *Dachshunds (Blastoff! Readers, Level 2: Awesome Pets)*. Bellwether Media, 2015.

WEBSITES

FACTSURFER

Factsurfer.com gives you a safe, fun way to find more information.

1. Go to www.factsurfer.com.
2. Enter "Dachshunds" into the search box and click 🔍
3. Select your book cover to see a list of related websites.

Glossary

animal shelter: a temporary home for animals.

instinct: an ability an animal is born with.

marathon: a running race of just over 26 miles (42.2 km).

mascot: an animal or character used as a symbol for a team or organization.

prey: animals who are being hunted.

snout: the nose of an animal.

spine: the bones that run along an animal's back.

Index

PHOTO CREDITS

The images in this book are reproduced through the courtesy of: Alamy: Interfoto 8. Shutterstock: Nynke van Holten 3; Masarik 4, 13BR, 13, 16, 26, 27; Yevhenii Slivin 6; Petrovichili 9; Liliya Kulianionak 10, 22; Csandand Kiss 13BL; Bigandt.com 13T; InGreen 14; Zanna Pesnina 17; Nicole Lienemann 18; Annette Shaff 19; otsphoto 20; dogboxstudio 22; Javier Brosch 23; Anetlanda 24; dogboxstudio 31.
Cover and page 1: SensorSpot/iStock. Paw prints: Maximillian Laschon/Shutterstock.

About the Author

Anna Davison writes about science, nature and health. She loves animals and has cared for dogs, cats, fish, frogs, and flatworms!